THE FALLEN SPACEMAN

Erik froze. He was looking straight into the eyes of the strangest little man he had ever seen. He had a small, shiny head with no hair at all, and wide, enormous eyes that reminded him of a sad puppy. Only for a moment was Erik frightened. Then a smile stretched his face. He almost laughed. Why, he had never expected the occupant of the robot to be so small! He was even smaller than his brother, and he had the saddest face Erik had ever seen.

And to think, Erik mused, *I was so afraid of him!*

"An exciting story of a boy who comes face to face with a helpless alien."

—*Instructor*

"The plot moves along quickly."
—*School Library Journal*

"A down-to-earth science-fiction story."
—*The New York Times*

THE
FALLEN
SPACEMAN
LEE HARDING

**Illustrations by
John and Ian Schoenherr**

A BANTAM SKYLARK BOOK®
TORONTO • NEW YORK • LONDON • SYDNEY • AUCKLAND

This low priced Bantam Book
has been completely reset in a type face
designed for easy reading, and was printed
from new plates. It contains the complete
text of the original hard-cover edition.
NOT ONE WORD HAS BEEN OMITTED.

RL3, 007-010

THE FALLEN SPACEMAN
A Bantam Skylark Book / published by arrangement with
Harper & Row, Publishers Inc.

PRINTING HISTORY
Harper & Row edition published October 1980
A Selection of Weekly Reader Children's Book Club
and Xerox Education Publications
Bantam Skylark edition / February 1982

Bantam Books are published by Bantam Books, Inc. Its trade-
mark, consisting of the words "Bantam Books" and the por-
trayal of a rooster, is Registered in U.S. Patent and Trademark
Office and in other countries. Marca Registrada. Bantam
Books, Inc., 666 Fifth Avenue, New York, New York 10103.

PRINTED IN THE UNITED STATES OF AMERICA

0 9 8 7 6

This book is dedicated to the memory of Jim Ellis—friend, patron and prince of publishers, who first encouraged this Spaceman to soar.

THE
FALLEN SPACEMAN

1

The alien starship circled Earth many times before the spaceman fell.

The people inside the starship looked a little like us, but they were different in many ways.

They came from another world in a distant part of the galaxy.

They were small, like children, with tiny arms and legs. They had large eyes and pale faces and no body hair at all, not even an eyelash. The tops of their heads were as smooth and as polished as apples.

Their voices were strange. To our ears their speech would sound more like music.

They moved around carefully. They were not very strong and their soft bones could be easily broken. But they had made many clever machines to do most of their work, and this gave them time to think and to play and otherwise enjoy themselves. In this way they were most like us.

They passed by our world on their way to another star. They were curious and decided to study Earth for a while. They swung their great starship into orbit and watched us through powerful telescopes.

They could not be seen from Earth. They had a way of making their starship invisible, so they could carry out their work undisturbed.

They drew maps of our world and their powerful cameras made a valuable record of our way of life. After several long days, they finished their study and resumed their journey.

They set course for a distant star. The whole ship began to vibrate as the mighty engines roared and pushed them away from Earth at a tremendous speed. In a matter of hours they would be clear of the solar system and heading in the direction of another star cluster.

But they made a terrible mistake. They forgot that Tyro was outside, working on the hull. . . .

Tyro was repairing a faulty camera when suddenly, without warning, he felt the great starship shudder under his feet.

He instantly recognized the deep vibration of

the atomic engines starting up. Puzzled, he wondered what the engineers were doing, and why he hadn't been called inside. It was dangerous to be working on the hull when the engines were being tested.

He glanced toward the enormous tail of the starship, where the great engines pointed at the stars. At that moment the hull shook underneath him and the rockets fired.

The stars blurred and spun about him. The shock of the starship taking off sent him spinning away into space, tumbling over and over like a wheel. He was knocked unconscious and could not stop his wild tumbling through the deep darkness of space.

In a matter of moments the starship was thousands of miles away. By the time they discovered one of their crew was missing, they would be in another part of the galaxy. In the meantime . . .

Tyro kept falling. Spinning and falling in no particular direction, while the bold blue Earth swam beneath him.

It was some time before he came to. He saw the stars spinning around outside his faceplate and knew that something terrible had happened.

He leaned forward in his safety harness and moved one of the control levers. Several small rockets fixed to the outside of his spacesuit fired for a few seconds. When they ceased, his wild tumbling had stopped. The stars had ceased their mad dance but there was nothing else for him to see.

Where was the starship? And why hadn't they come back for him?

Tyro shivered. Never before had he felt so completely alone . . . and afraid.

His spacesuit was enormous. It was as tall as a five-story building and he sat inside it, in the center, protected by his safety webbing, like a spider in his web.

He was small and weak, but his spacesuit had great power. It was built like a small starship. In front of him was a control panel with many dials and switches, and behind it was a small computer that helped him to control his movements.

His spacesuit was powered by a small atomic engine. It was strong enough to move a starship into orbit or push a mountain to one side. There were small rocket motors built into the arms and legs, and by firing them carefully, he was able to move around in space.

He moved another lever. Then another. The spacesuit began to turn around. The stars moved to one side and the great blue globe of Earth appeared in his faceplate.

An aching sadness crept over him when he realized he was lost. What would he do if the starship did not return? He could not stay up

4

here forever! His air would run out in a few more hours.

He tried not to think about that. Instead he thought of himself, drifting idly around Earth, waiting for a rescue that might never come.

Better to take his chances on the unknown world below! If he could reach it in safety, he would be able to keep alive until the starship returned—if it ever returned.

What would the air be like down there? he wondered. If it was unsuitable for breathing he would die an equally painful death. But at least he would have tried.

His head was clear now. He studied the control panel carefully. He had made up his mind to go down . . . and take his chances. There was no time to waste—every moment that ticked away used up a little more of his precious air supply.

It was a long way down to Earth. The descent would take several hours, and there was much that worried him about the journey.

He would fall at a great speed—so fast that his spacesuit would be burned up like a meteorite if he didn't use his rockets carefully. At the very last moment the computer would reverse them and direct their energy toward the ground, breaking his fall. With luck he would make a safe landing with fuel to spare.

The computer plotted a safe downward course.

Tyro sat back and waited while it took over the controls and got the strange journey under way.

The huge spacesuit dipped slowly toward Earth. The beautiful blue world swam out of view. All he could see were the solemn stars.

He felt his shoulder rockets fire, gently pushing him *down*. He began to fall feetfirst and very fast.

Tyro was frightened for the first few minutes. But after a while he got used to the strange feeling and relaxed in his safety harness.

He thought about the unknown world below. He didn't know much about Earth. He was a cameraman, not a scientist. All he knew about Earth was what he had picked up as gossip around the ship.

It was said that the people of Earth were large and warlike, and that they had loud voices and were always fighting among themselves.

He would have to find somewhere to hide while he waited for the starship, and that might not be so easy. But for the moment all he was concerned with was a safe landing.

Faster and faster fell the spaceman. The Earth grew large beneath him and nudged into view outside his faceplate—blue and bold and beautiful.

Soon the Earth had pushed everything else

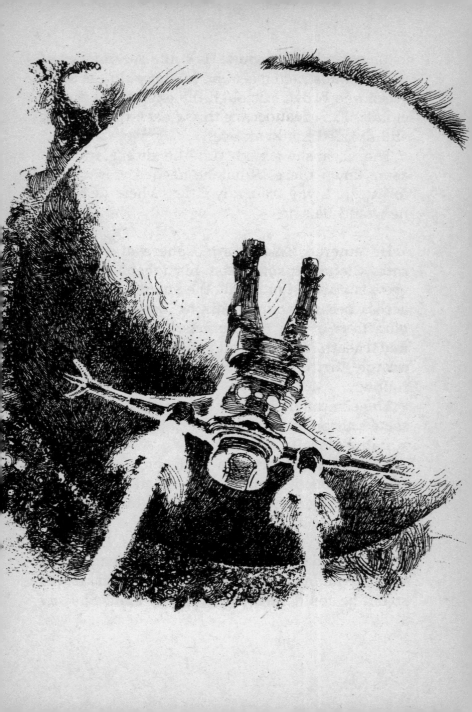

aside and filled his view. He could see patches of white clouds racing around it. He could see land, green and brown, through the gaps in the fleecy clouds. The great oceans threw back the sunlight and dazzled his weak eyes.

The oceans worried him—he didn't want to come down there! What he needed was a deep forest, far away from any cities, where he hoped he would be safe.

He entered Earth's atmosphere at a terrific rate. Clouds rushed past his faceplate and it grew suddenly hot inside the spacesuit. He sped across oceans and mountains, forests and jungles, deserts and rain forests. Cities flashed by underneath his spacesuit's gigantic feet. He saw all the Earth, but too fast for his tired eyes to follow.

The computer saw and recorded *everything*. It sorted through this information, looking for a suitable place to land.

Tyro could never have made such a swift descent without its help, and he relied upon it now to choose the right place for him to hide from the warlike people of Earth.

Faster and faster he fell. Inside the spacesuit it was like an oven. Tyro prayed to his gods. It was so hot he could hardly breathe. He glanced away

8

from the controls and out through the faceplate. He was over land again, and falling at a steep angle toward a wooded mountain range.

Will I make it alive? he wondered. The heat was burning him up. His eyes stung and his skin had begun to dry up.

Two miles up and falling! The wind buffeted his spacesuit like an angry fist.

The forest, rich and green, raced up from below in his faceplate. The computer was guiding him toward a small clearing in the trees.

The bare ground reached up for him. Tyro felt a warm glow of relief. He closed his eyes and whispered a last prayer.

He was only a few hundred feet above the forest when the computer fired the braking rockets. Flashes of fire flared at the feet of the spacesuit, slowing its dangerous fall.

But something inside the computer slipped. It corrected too much. The blackened spacesuit came to a sudden halt in midair, jiggling around as though a giant, invisible hand were shaking it.

Tyro was thrown forward—only his safety harness saved him from dashing his head against the control panel. He looked about, wild-eyed with surprise. *Whatever was happening?* ...

The spacesuit danced across the sky like something gone mad, rockets blazing. The fall had been checked, but the powerful surge of energy had thrown the spacesuit wildly off course. Now it cavorted drunkenly above the trees like a dotty old man.

Tyro saw what was happening. He reached forward to take manual control, but the panel would not respond; the levers were stiff and lifeless in his tiny hands!

Gradually the spacesuit steadied as the dazed computer realized what had happened. But by then it was too late to avoid disaster.

Tyro almost made it. The topmost branches of the trees were level with his faceplate when the spacesuit finally straightened up. And then . . .

The rockets coughed and died. The last drop of precious rocket fuel had been used up trying to stop the wild tumbling of the spacesuit.

The spaceman *fell*.

The air screamed past his faceplate. Tyro pressed an emergency button, and a second safety harness snapped around him, pinning him down.

He closed his eyes and waited. The ground rushed up to meet him. The tearing, crashing noise outside rose to a dreadful roar.

The spacesuit slammed into the ground with its speed unchecked. The shock rattled every bone in Tyro's body. The spacesuit toppled over and buried its great helmeted head in the ground. Tyro passed out. But his last conscious thought was that he was down at last.

And alive.

2

Erik and Stephen saw the spaceman fall. They were playing by the creek when it happened.

At first they heard a far-off, high-pitched whine. It sounded like some sort of aircraft, only different from anything similar they had ever heard. In a moment it had grown into a desperate rushing sound that made them look up.

The sky seemed to split open. The noise grew into a frightful roar.

They saw something small and dark and smoking streak down from the sky. It crashed into the forest, not far away from where they stood.

The strange object was not stopped by the treetops. They could hear it tearing a way down through the trees. A second later the ground shook beneath their feet. Birds flew screaming into the sky and the whole forest was in an uproar.

Gradually the air grew still again, and Erik looked at his younger brother. "Now what on Earth was *that*?" he said.

Stephen shrugged and looked uneasy. He was only seven and there were many things he didn't understand. He rubbed his nose and stared at the trees, a little scared by what they had seen.

"Could have been a meteorite," Erik said, thoughtfully. "One of those falling stars."

"What if it's a UFO?" Stephen said.

An unidentified flying object? Erik nodded. Well, why not? You read enough about them— maybe they *did* exist. Some people called them flying saucers. Neither of them had ever seen a UFO, but they *might* exist. It was rather like ghosts, Erik thought—you had to see one before you were convinced.

The falling object had been smoking, so it must have burned up in the atmosphere. Maybe it was only a meteorite, after all.

"Come on," he said, urging his little brother to join him. "Let's go have a look at it. . . ."

Erik set off at a run. Stephen was slow to follow. He was uneasy about stepping into the forest, and doubtful of what they might find there. He didn't share his older brother's interest in outer space . . . but he didn't like being left alone, either.

"Wait for me, Erik," he called out. And ràn after him.

But they did not run for long. The slope of the field grew steep. Their pace had slowed to a walk well before they reached the edge of the forest.

It was dark and gloomy among the tightly packed trees.

"Why don't we go back and get Dad?" Stephen wanted to know.

"Don't be a scaredy," Erik said. "I bet it's only a small meteorite, that's all." He took his brother's hand and stepped cautiously into the forest.

Erik sniffed the air. It was heavy with the smell of scorched earth. The object must have been very hot when it reached the ground. Stephen pressed close against his brother. "I wish Dad was here," he kept saying. But Dad was some distance away, back with Mum at their summer house.

Ahead they could see where the falling object had torn a great cleft in the trees. Erik hurried forward, dragging his little brother behind. They squeezed through some dense ferns and then . . .

They stood on the edge of the wide clearing newly carved from the forest. At the center of the clearing a huge blackened object lay crumpled on the ground. It looked like a giant made of metal, stranded on the floor of the forest and burned black.

"*What is it?*" Stephen whispered.

"I don't know," Erik replied. "We'll have to get a closer look. . . ."

Stephen pulled back into the shadows. "You go, Erik," he said. "I'll wait here."

As Erik drew closer he saw that the object was shaped roughly like a man—seventy feet tall!

Erik could make out enormous arms and legs and a strange, ugly head. The huge legs ended in great treads, like a tractor, and each one was the size of a car.

If this thing was truly a spacesuit, he thought, then it must belong to a creature so big that it could only have come from another world!

Another world . . .

"Erik," Stephen called out from the edge of the ragged clearing. "I want to go home now. I want to tell Dad." He looked forlorn and frightened hunched down in the undergrowth. He didn't want to get any closer to the fallen spaceman.

Erik waved him to be quiet. "In a minute," he called back. "I just want to get a little closer. . . ."

He waited a moment, but the giant gave no sign that it could move.

What if the . . . the creature inside had been

15

killed by the fall? Erik wondered. Or what if he was only unconscious?

He frowned and looked up at the great cleft torn through the forest. It seemed unlikely that anyone could have survived such a dreadful fall. And yet . . . *and yet* . . .

He crept cautiously around the great helmeted head. He wasn't surprised to find a faceplate on the other side. It was mostly covered with dirt and twigs where the head had plowed into the ground.

ng and the

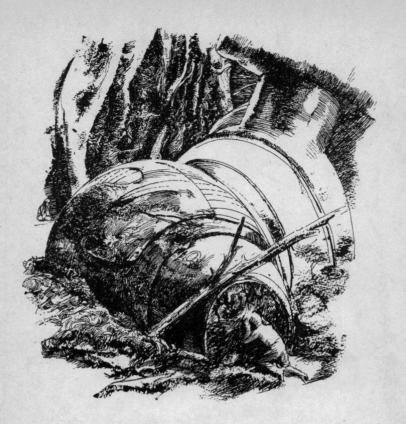

He took a deep breath and leaned forward, scraping some of the dirt away with nervous fingers. The glass was still warm but not so hot it could not be touched.

When most of the dirt had been removed, he bent closer and peered through the glass.

It took a few moments for his eyes to adjust. The faceplate was dark, like sunglasses, but after a while he thought he saw something moving inside. . . .

3

For a long time after he came to, Tyro was too sore to move. His chest was badly bruised where his safety harness had held him down—but it *had* saved his life.

He wondered how much time had passed since the crash . . . and how much precious air he had left.

He touched a lever and the two safety harnesses whipped out of sight. He sat up and rubbed his aching arms and legs. He could feel the pull of gravity, and from the angle of the spacesuit, he realized it had fallen on one side.

He couldn't see a thing through the faceplate. The helmet had plowed deeply into the ground, making it impossible to see anything outside. Inside the spacesuit it was like twilight.

He moved a switch and was relieved when a weak artificial light flooded the inside of the spacesuit. It seemed that not everything had been damaged by the fall.

Gradually he became aware of an unusual quiet inside the spacesuit. There was not even the soft purr of the control computer to break the silence.

The computer. Now he remembered. . . .

The computer had made a mistake, and that mistake had almost cost him his life. And if the spacesuit was damaged beyond repair it could *still* cost him.

Tyro fiddled with the controls. Nothing happened. He tapped out an urgent message directed to the computer. Again, there was no response. He might well be enjoying the luxury of being alive, but his spacesuit seemed quite dead.

Just when he was about to give in to despair, there was a soft whir from the control panel. A few weak lights lit up. One of them showed COMPUTER READY.

Tyro breathed a deep sigh of relief and settled back in his seat.

"All right," he said, in his strange musical speech, "how bad is it? Let me have a full report."

There was a delay of several seconds before the

computer replied, in a mechanical copy of Tyro's voice.

There has been . . . some damage, it croaked. Its voice coil had been badly damaged by the fall, but it managed to get by.

It will take some time . . . to find out . . . how badly.

"Be as fast as you can," he ordered. "But first, let me have a report on the air of this world—is it safe for me to breathe?"

He sat back to wait, nervously twisting his tiny fingers together.

The computer gave its report a few minutes later, having taken in a sample of the outside air and studied it carefully.

You may breathe the outside air, it said, *but only for a short time. A little of it, mixed with your own, will extend your life by many hours, but it will also make you dizzy and unable to perform the most simple tasks. It has too much oxygen. Too much of it will kill you. . . .*

It was just as Tyro had feared. This world could not support him. He listened with growing despair to what the computer said.

You have enough air in reserve, it went on, *to last seven hours. At the end of that time . . .*

Tyro told the computer to be quiet. He knew only too well what awaited him at the end of that time: a lingering death breathing the atmosphere of this unknown planet.

"Prepare a full report on the workings of this spacesuit," he ordered. I want to know *how* much damage has been done."

The computer whirred quietly to itself as it went about this important business.

Tyro sat back, weak and sore. His senses reached out and made contact with the outside world.

The forest felt warm and kind. Nothing to fear out there. And yet . . .

There was something else. Something that moved. He could *feel* it. And it was coming closer.

A shadow fell across his faceplate, shutting out what little light found its way in through the dust and dirt that covered the glass.

He heard scraping sounds. Something was scratching away at the dirt covering his faceplate.

Tyro tensed and sat forward. There was nothing he could do! There might be some dangerous animal outside, struggling to get in. Given time, his spacesuit would repair itself and he would be more than a match for any life form on this planet. But not *now*. Not when he was still crippled and helpless!

The scraping continued. A few inches of sunlight crept into the spacesuit. And Tyro saw large white fingers nervously scraping the dirt away.

Tyro was astonished. The fingers were so like his own, only *much* longer. A wave of relief washed over him. No animal, then, but a creature like himself. One of the leading race of bipeds who ruled this planet . . . and perhaps more dangerous than any four-footed animal.

He held his breath and waited while the busy fingers completed their work.

The glass of the faceplate was polarized. He could see clearly through it, but a person outside would have great difficulty looking in.

The scraping stopped. There was a long pause and then the shadow moved again, blotting out the sun.

A strange face peered in through the faceplate.

Tyro shuddered and crouched low in his seat. The stranger's face was bigger than his own. The face was longer and a great thatch of hair sprouted from the head. The eyes were wide and startled. The stranger looked into the faceplate for a moment and then disappeared.

A moment later the strange face moved back in front of the faceplate. Tyro could feel great waves of uneasiness reaching into his mind.

For a moment he managed a weak smile. It seemed that the alien outside was as worried as he was!

He wondered if the stranger could see him, or

whether the polarized glass would make it too dark inside the helmet to see.

The face was close enough for Tyro to see the color of the eyes. They were a deep and lustrous blue, a color quite rare to Tyro's people. The skin was dark—much darker than Tyro's, whose people lived most of their life in deep space. Their skin was pale because of the artificial light they used on board their great starships.

They stared at each other through the faceplate. A strange silence drew them together. And then, when another few moments had passed, the strange face pulled back slowly from the darkened glass. It disappeared to one side, leaving the sunlight to come streaming in.

Tyro sat quite still for some time, waiting for his wildly beating heart to calm down, and for the computer to deliver its final report.

But he could not erase from his mind the image of that strange and disturbing alien face.

4

Erik felt strange all over. He stepped back from the enormous helmeted head of the fallen space-man and looked around in a dazed manner. He felt dizzy. He wondered if this was because of some strange fumes escaping from the spacesuit, or the result of peering too deeply into the dark-ened faceplate.

He thought he had seen something shadowy moving on the other side of the faceplate, inside the spacesuit. But he couldn't be sure.

"Erik, are you coming now?" Stephen called out.

Erik nodded, a little vaguely. He still felt lightheaded. But there was nothing more to see. It was time to go back home and tell Dad what they had found.

He crept away from the fallen spaceman and back to where his brother waited.

"Come on," he said, in a hushed whisper, *"let's get going. . . ."*

Dad was working in his shed when they arrived.

He collected rocks, and the walls of the shed held hundreds of them. Each one was neatly tagged and numbered.

Some of them were very beautiful, but not so as you would notice on the outside. You had to cut them open to see that.

They were millions of years old, their father said. And when he sliced them open with a special saw, you could see how they were patterned inside, some like seashells, with beautiful whorls of color. Who would ever have thought that a little old rock could be so marvelous inside?

He was at his workbench when they rushed in, panting from their long run.

"Dad!" Erik cried. "There's a fallen spaceman in the forest! He just came down. We *saw* him. Over past the creek! Only a little way into the trees. . . ."

Dad looked up from his work. He had a kind

face and a short, well-trimmed beard. His eyes were gentle and he looked out at them through gold-rimmed glasses. But his face was stern.

Erik could see that he didn't know whether or not to believe them. But he had heard a great noise rip open the sky and felt a crash. The impact had shaken the shed like a small earthquake.

"A spaceman?" he asked. "Are you sure? It seemed to pack quite a wallop. . . ."

Erik jumped up and down with excitement. "It's true! We saw him! Didn't we, Stephen?"

His younger brother nodded in agreement.

"And he's so *big!*" Erik stretched wide his arms, trying to give some idea of the monstrous size of the spacesuit. "You've never seen anything like him!"

Their father looked thoughtful. He put aside his polishing cloths and stood up. "Are you sure it wasn't . . . some sort of satellite? Or a meteorite?"

Erik shook his head vigorously. "No, it's a *spaceman*. You'll see. Come and we'll show you. . . ."

"All right," he said, giving in to their enthusiasm at last. "Let's have a look at it. . . ."

Erik showed the way. Their clothes were soon damp again from the moisture on the bushes, but they did not mind. They were too concerned with finding the fallen spaceman.

Dad gasped when he saw the great cleft in the trees.

"Only a little way now," Erik whispered, without thinking it strange that his voice should become so hushed when they were so close to the giant.

"Move quietly," their father cautioned. On the off chance that there was something alive inside the object, he didn't think it should be disturbed.

They came to a halt near the edge of the shattered clearing. The fallen spaceman lay where they had last seen it, a broken heap of blackened metal still cooling in the sunlight.

"You *see*," Erik whispered, triumphantly, "I told you it was a *spaceman*. . . ."

Their father raised a finger to his lips and hushed them. "Wait here," he whispered, and stepped forward alone into the clearing.

It took but a moment for him to see that the children had indeed been telling the truth. This was no melted meteorite or a stricken weather satellite. It was shaped like a man and it must have been all of seventy feet tall!

Could this be some sort of joke? he wondered, or the remains of some secret experiment gone wrong?

But the closer he moved, the more likely it

29

seemed that the creature inside this cumbersome metal spacesuit had come from another world. A world of *giants*.

He circled the spaceman warily. It had fallen on its right side, just as Erik had told him, and the great head was half buried in the ground.

He moved around until he could see the faceplate his son had scraped clear.

He waited a moment before bending down to peer into the darkened faceplate. It reminded him of the deep tint of sunglasses. Perhaps it was made that way, he thought, so that whoever was inside could see *out* clearly enough, but nobody could look *in*.

Of course he was only half right. The special glass in Tyro's faceplate had been designed to filter out the raw, blinding energy of the stars, not to keep strangers from seeing inside.

He stared into the faceplate for several long minutes. Once or twice he thought he saw something move on the other side, but he couldn't be sure. After a while he shrugged and stood up.

While their father was examining the strange faceplate, the boys crept forward and studied the back of the spacesuit.

Erik gave a tiny cry of delight when he discovered a small opening in the blackened metal.

It was tiny—a crack only a few inches wide—but it looked like some sort of entrance hatch, knocked open by the fall.

"I wonder what's inside?" Erik whispered. He realized he was staring at a doorway into another world and a different way of life.

He found that by forcing the metal there was enough space for one of them to crawl through.

Stephen guessed what was in his mind. "Don't go in, Erik," he urged. "Dad will be angry if he finds out. . . ."

But their father was busy around the other side. There was time for a quick peek. With a little effort he managed to squeeze himself half-way through the narrow opening.

It was dark inside—and warm. The air smelt stuffy and strange. Somewhere close by he could hear the faint whir of machinery. As his eyes adjusted to the gloom he discovered there was a weak light inside.

He gave an extra heave and the door moved another inch. And another. He squeezed the rest of his body inside.

He found himself in a chamber, turned side-ways by the fall. It was quite large—and empty. The walls shone with an eerie radiance and the sunlight that filtered in through the opening he had forced revealed a curious ladder on his right.

Erik began to have grave doubts. What if this

was not a spacesuit but a gigantic *robot* sent to Earth to gather information for possible invaders?

The chamber could be some kind of entrance hatch for . . . servicemen. It was much too lage to be part of a spacesuit. And yet—how could he be sure? Only by crawling along that ladder and discovering where it led to. . . .

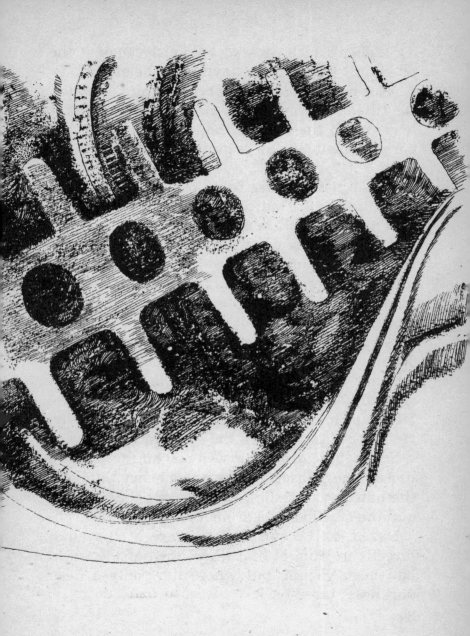

Stephen's face pressed anxiously against the opening. "Can you see anything?" he asked.

"Not much. Just an empty room and a ladder. It's tilted sideways at the moment, but I think it leads up to the top. To the head. And there's a curious smell. The air is quite strange. I feel a bit dizzy. . . ."

"Then you'd better come out. Quickly," Stephen urged. "If Dad catches you in there . . ."

"I'm coming," Erik answered. He couldn't wait to tell his father what he had discovered inside the spacesuit or robot or whatever. He moved toward the open hatch . . . and swayed dizzily against the side of the spacesuit. He felt suddenly sleepy.

"Come *on*, come *on*," Stephen kept calling. There was rising concern in his voice.

"I'm . . . coming," Erik mumbled. The words seemed to hang from his lips like heavy bubbles. He could hardly move. His legs were like jelly. He reached out toward the open hatch. . . .

Somewhere nearby unseen machinery whirred like an angry insect. There was a heavy thud and the hatch swung shut, blotting out the sunlight and the startled face of his brother.

Dazed, Erik continued to stare at that spot directly in front of him where the outside world had been visible, but where now only a deep darkness stared back.

It took a few moments for his muddled mind to figure out what had happened.

The doorway had shut and he was trapped inside the spacesuit.

Inside the spacesuit . . .

He leaned weakly against the metal side of the spacesuit and called out. "Dad, can you hear me? Dad . . . get me out. *Please get me out! . . .*"

He could feel the panic unwinding inside him. It left him cold and shaking, in spite of the warmth inside the spacesuit.

He banged his weak fists against the metal side. But they were timid blows—his strength was slipping away.

"Help me," Erik pleaded. *"Please help me."* But his words were lost in the darkness.

Stephen was terrified when the hatch closed, sealing his brother inside. He called out several times, but there was no answer.

He ran around the other side of the spacesuit to tell their father what had happened, and they hurried around to the back of the spacesuit. Stephen searched all along the blackened surface, trying to find the doorway. But he found no trace at all.

"Erik—can you hear me?" Dad called out.

There was no reply. Perhaps the metal was too thick for any sound to penetrate.

He swore and pounded his fists against the blackened surface. And still there was no reply.

Oh, my God, he thought. *Whatever has happened to him?* He cast a desperate look at his younger son. "Are you sure he's in here, Stephen?"

Stephen nodded. "He *did* go in there, Dad. He really *did.*"

Dad leaned heavily against the fallen spaceman. *I mustn't panic,* he thought. *I have to find a way to get him out before . . . before he runs out of air and suffocates.* It wasn't a pleasant thought.

He was torn two ways—how could he run back to the house and get help but leave his son alone, trapped inside this strange machine from another world?

He was still trying to decide what to do when the fallen spaceman *moved.*

5

It had taken a long time for Tyro to get his spacesuit working. The fall had caused a lot of damage. But the computer checked everything out and made the necessary repairs, and when it had fixed everything it could, it told Tyro it was ready to move.

Tyro was pleased to hear the spacesuit whirring and humming for the first time since the fall. He was still uneasy about the sudden appearance of the Earth people. The first one had gone away and then a much bigger one had appeared.

Tyro shivered when he remembered how scared he had been when the huge, strange face had peered in through the faceplate.

He was much bigger than Tyro. And probably much stronger. Without his spacesuit Tyro would be helpless against such a giant. He was anxious to have his spacesuit working again, so that he need not fear these strangers.

The people outside had made no move to harm him, but there was no sense in taking chances. If they knew how small and helpless he was . . .

But everything was working now. There was no longer any need to feel afraid. He would soon be far away from here and hiding somewhere else.

He had a six-hour supply of air left. If the starship hadn't returned in that time, then he would have to open his helmet and let the unhealthy outside air in.

How long could he expect to breathe that air and remain alive? The computer could only guess. *About an hour,* it had said. It would take that long for the oxygen-rich air to strangle him. Long before that, of course, his body would begin to break down.

Tyro shuddered. It was not a pleasant thought.

When everything was ready to go, he cautiously touched the control levers. It wouldn't do to feed in too much power all at once. He would have to ease the spacesuit gently back to work.

His hands were soft and weak, but when he used the controls they became strong. The huge spacesuit faithfully followed his movements like a shadow. When it moved, there would be nothing on Earth that could stop it. But he would have to be careful not to harm anyone. It would not do for the Earth people to think him dangerous. . . .

A bright red light suddenly winked on the panel. Tyro was puzzled. It was a signal that the entrance hatch was open.

He felt a sudden stab of alarm. It must have been jarred open by the fall . . . and the outside air would have been leaking in ever since. No wonder he felt so strange in the head!

How had the computer missed it?

He was about to lean forward and press the switch that closed it manually, when the red light winked off.

The hatch was closed again.

Tyro breathed a sigh of relief. But just to be sure, he asked the computer to make a double check.

A second later the computer replied that all was well. The door *had* been jarred open but it was now closed.

Tyro nodded . . . and then frowned. The computer was making too many mistakes.

It was time to begin testing his damaged spacesuit. First he moved his great right hand. He fitted his own into a metal glove on the right of the control panel. Tiny wires in the glove made contact with his flesh and carried his movements to the computer, where they were coded and fed to the mighty engines. And all this happened in the smallest fraction of a second.

Tyro flexed his fingers inside the glove. Outside, the enormous right hand of the spacesuit copied his movements. It slowly raised itself a few inches from the floor of the forest and . . .

Stephen was first to see the spaceman move. "Dad!" he called out. "Look—over there! It's *moving*. . . ."

They crouched down near the edge of the clearing and waited.

The body of the spaceman remained still. But one hand had begun to move in a strangely human manner.

The huge fingers opened and closed, opened and closed, in a curious flexing gesture. The effect was quite startling.

Stephen huddled close to his father. "Dad, *what's happening? Is it—*"

Dad hushed him to be quiet. He was sick with fear now that the spaceman had stirred and was coming back to life. It seemed impossible that they could save Erik.

They continued to watch in wide-eyed wonder as the spaceman moved. . . .

The great right hand of the spaceman rose several feet from the ground. There was a loud whirring of machinery and then the other hand came into view. The giant held them aloft for several minutes, turning them over and around, as if he were inspecting them. Then very slowly they relaxed and came back to rest on the ground.

Stephen and his father listened with growing alarm to the deep growling sounds coming from inside the spacesuit.

"It sounds like a . . . a robot," Stephen whispered.

His father nodded, eyes narrowed. It did indeed. In which case his son might be safe for a while. The alien robot might not know he was inside. But it was such a slim chance. . . .

Of course, they were only close to the truth. The spacesuit was a mechanical being, true enough—but what they couldn't know was that inside this huge robot there was a small creature from another world, who looked a little like themselves and who was much more frightened of the situation than they!

It was time to get help. There was nothing they could do here, nothing at all. And they would have to hurry if they were to cut their way into the spaceman and rescue Erik before the robot began to move around.

At that moment there came a great groaning sound and the spaceman sat up.

The effect was quite strange. The bottom half of his metal body didn't move an inch, but from the waist up it rose with alarming suddenness. And that wasn't all. . . .

The spaceman began to *creak*. It was the kind of sound you would expect machinery to make when there wasn't enough oil on the bearings. The sound cut through the silence of the forest like a scythe.

Very slowly, the great helmeted head began to rotate. It moved around like a run-down turntable, with a strange jerky rhythm.

Three times it rotated. They could hear the busy little motors turning it around . . . and around . . . and around.

On the fourth rotation it came to a sudden stop. The darkened faceplate was pointing in their direction.

It seemed to be watching them, and they were too scared to move. Father and son were frozen to the spot.

Tyro studied the Earth people. One was quite large, the other much smaller. The tall one would be an adult, he thought. Such height made the little alien feel uncomfortable. He had never seen anyone so big in all his life, and he was glad to have his spacesuit working again. For a while there he had felt like a lost child, small and weak and lonely. *His* home and *his* parents were millions of miles away . . . and he might never see them again.

He had decided it was best not to make contact with the Earth people. He remembered starship gossip that said they were a very warlike race. Indeed, even from this distance the two natives looked rather fierce. And yet . . . he could feel no hostility directed at him. Only fear. This gave him confidence.

Tyro could read feelings as easily as Earth people read words. It was as natural for him as speech is for them. In this way his people were *very* different from the people of Earth.

So Tyro was puzzled. He did not feel that these people would harm him, but he thought it would be best to leave this area as fast as he could. He had no way of knowing what the rest of the natives would be like. Perhaps so far he had only been lucky.

The Earth people had not moved from the edge of the clearing. They seemed to be watching and waiting for something. He could sense their fear and felt sorry for them. He wanted to call out, *Do not be afraid. I will not harm you.* But of course they would never understand his strange musical speech.

Tyro made up his mind. It was time to get moving. He gave the computer full control and sat back in his seat. To wait.

In the brief silence before the atomic motors roared into life, Tyro thought he heard a strange sound. It was unlike anything he had ever heard, and it seemed to come from the entrance hatch, below and behind him.

Had something crawled inside his spacesuit when the hatch was open? Perhaps a small rodent, or some other forest animal?

For a moment he was alarmed. Then he shrugged his small shoulders. No need to worry. The air inside the spacesuit would soon put it to sleep. He was in no danger.

The sound was repeated again—a soft, hollow sound, like a child crying.

Tyro frowned. He was about to climb out of his protective webbing when the spacesuit roared louder than before. The control room shook and shuddered and the giant spacesuit lurched to its feet.

"Get back!" Dad cried. He pushed his son ahead of him, deeper into the forest.

The fallen spaceman stood up awkwardly, its great feet churning up the ground, showering the nearby trees with dirt and broken branches.

Strange sounds came from inside the spaceman, sounds like a truck with a broken gearbox. It waved its arms around like a madman.

Inside the spacesuit, Tyro groaned. All was not well!

"Stop it!" he said to the computer. "You are feeding too much power to the treads! We want to move *quietly* away from here, not so loud that the whole world can hear us!"

The computer croaked out a reply. *My . . . mistake. There is still . . . much work . . . to be done.*

Tyro groaned again. "Just get us away from here, that's all! And do it *quietly*. We've drawn enough attention already from these curious natives."

He hoped that the computer, although damaged, would be able to perform the simple task of directing them away from the clearing. But the spacesuit roared and lurched toward the trees.

"Not that way!" Tyro cried. The damaged computer didn't reply.

The spacesuit crashed through the trees, sending them crashing to either side. Its great treads dug deeply into the ground and threw up a shower of dark earth, almost hiding it from view.

The enormous arms of the spacesuit were spread wide, pushing even the tallest trees to one side. The spacesuit roared on, cutting a deep tunnel through the dark forest.

It was out of control!

6

"*My God,*" Dad exclaimed. He didn't wait a moment longer, but picking his small son up in his arms, he turned around and raced back through the forest toward the house.

If only there was time enough to save Erik!

He would have to call the police . . . and then the army. Only the army could hope to stop such a giant. But they would have to be careful—if they frightened the alien and it fought back, they would be endangering the life of his son.

He tried not to think what would happen if they refused to believe him, and how much time would be wasted while he argued with them. If only there had been other witnesses! All they'd have would be the word of one frightened father and a seven-year-old boy.

So far the spaceman had made no move to harm them, but its actions might change for the worse if it found itself threatened. And by now he was convinced it was a robot.

But time enough to worry about that later, he thought. First they had to catch up with it!

When they reached the house Mum was waiting outside. She had sensed, from a distance, that something was wrong. She saw the terrible look on Dad's face and stood aside as he raced up the porch steps.

Stephen took his Mum's hand and dragged her inside to where Dad was shouting into the telephone. They stood back and listened in silence.

"Listen," he said, his voice high and angry. "I don't care *what* you think—that monstrous machine has kidnapped my son! I tell you I *saw* it. Just send help over here—*fast*. If they're fast enough, they might even get a glimpse of it before—how big? Good heavens, man—taller than two or three houses, so help me! Yes, yes, I know. I understand! But this is *urgent*. If your men don't take a month of Sundays to get here, we might be able to find a way to stop it. No, it can't have come from anywhere on Earth. It's too *big*. Look, can we *please* stop wasting time? Just get a car over here—that thing's got our son inside!"

At first the police wouldn't listen to him. They thought he was some sort of nut, a crackpot. It was a joke, a hoax. But Dad didn't let up. He hung on to the phone and argued and pleaded with them for many long minutes until they finally agreed to send someone over.

"And for God's sake hurry!" he said, slamming the phone down angrily.

He turned to face his wife's suddenly frightened face. It was drained of color. His spirits fell. He went over and put his arms around her. "I'm sorry, Anne. I would have told you first, only I didn't want to waste a moment getting through to them. You do understand, don't you?"

She nodded and then looked at him with a shocked expression. "I . . . I just can't believe what I just heard, John. What *really* happened out there with the boys? I heard you mention something alien, something bigger than three houses. And it's got Erik inside?"

He got her to sit down while he explained what had happened. Stephen waited by the door. "Will they be long, Dad?" he asked.

Dad looked grim. "I hope not. I certainly hope not. . . ."

The low-gear sound of a car came up the driveway. They hurried outside to meet it.

It was a police car, all right. Stephen felt relieved that they had come. Now they would soon be able to get Erik away from the giant!

Dad quickly opened the back door of the police car and climbed in.

There were two policemen in the front. They nodded good-day. " 'Lo, John," the older one said. He was Officer Binns. He had a long, sad sort of face and not much sense of humor. He took everything seriously. The other man was Officer Pauls; he was more easy-going.

"Now then," Officer Binns began, clearing his throat, "perhaps you could show me the whereabouts of this 'ere giant spaceman of yours?"

"Head down the road a bit," Dad said. "Near the edge of the forest there. And for heaven's sake *hurry*! It could be miles away by now. . . ."

Officer Binns nodded, like someone being kind to a mental patient. "I say, John, this isn't some sort er gag, is it? You're not—"

Dad glared at him. "It's got my son" was all he said in a leaden voice.

Stephen and his mother climbed in beside him and the police car roared away down the driveway.

They picked up speed when they reached the road. Officer Binns kept asking Dad questions about the fallen spaceman. He told him all he could remember. And then . . .

The road shuddered underneath them. They

could feel it shaking the body of the car like a great wind.

"What . . . ?" Officer Pauls said. He was driving, and the wheel was fighting him like a demon. "What the *blazes* . . . ?"

The car skidded to a stop in the middle of the dirt road. The ground still shook. They looked at each other dazedly. Only Stephen and his father didn't look surprised.

On the left, something huge crashed through the trees and out onto the road. The air screamed as the spaceman came into view, his great long legs crossing the road in one mighty step. The enormous treads churned up the road on either side, showering the police car with dirt and stones.

"Good 'eavens," Officer Binns cried. He could not believe his eyes!

Only for a moment did the spaceman tower over them. Then it crashed into the trees on the other side of the road, its great arms held wide and pushing and bending the trees aside. The ground thundered as it moved, and flights of birds rose screaming into the sky marking where it had been. It sounded as though some dreadful war was being waged in the forest.

Dad was out of the car like a shot when the dust had settled. A pocket camera dangled from his wrist and he ran to where the spaceman had crossed the road.

He stood before the great gap carved through the trees and swung the camera up to his eye and quickly took several photographs.

He was firing blindly. He couldn't see anything moving down that dark tunnel, but he hoped the camera would capture some image, however

vague, of the spaceman. He needed *proof*—anything at all that would hasten the rescue of his son.

"Did you get anything?" Officer Pauls was asking. Dad shook his head. "I . . . I'm not sure. Maybe—maybe not. For a moment there, I could have sworn I saw it. But it moves so darned *fast*!" He looked at his pocket camera. "We'll have to wait and see how these turn out. Find a fast-printing lab in the city. . . ."

Officer Binns looked very grave. "An' you say that your son's inside that thing?"

Dad nodded.

Officer Binns straightened his shoulders. He seemed to have arrived at an important decision. "Come along then—no sense 'angin' around 'ere. We'll have to get movin' if we're ever to catch up to that thing. . . ."

They hurried back to the car.

"But we can't chase it through the forest," Mum protested.

Officer Binns nodded. "Indeed we can't. Helicopters is what we'll be needin' . . . an' lots of 'em. We won't find any around this neck of the woods."

They climbed into the police car and it roared back to the house.

"What's going to happen now?" Stephen wanted to know.

"We're going to the city," Dad explained. "Officer Binns, Officer Pauls . . . and me. You will have to stay here and look after Mum. . . ."

The city was more than twenty miles away—a half an hour drive. Dad hoped that once they were there it would only be a matter of time before they found the help they needed. But every minute took the giant spaceman farther away!

They dropped Stephen and his mother off at the house. Then the police car took off down the highway as though driven by a madman.

It was the beginning of a wild race against time.

It was less than an hour before the news was heard on radio and television.

Stephen and his mother had been waiting anxiously, eyes fixed upon their television set. Dad had phoned in briefly on his way to some army headquarters, only a short time ago. Everything was all right, he had told them. Alone he might never have convinced anybody, but the testimony of the two policemen had helped him to break through the curtain of red tape and disbelief.

A grim-faced announcer stared back at them from the television screen. The color had washed out of his features and they knew that this was no fault of their color set. He looked very much the frightened newsman.

"We interrupt this program," he said, "for an urgent announcement.

"Earlier today, an unidentified flying object was seen to fall in the mountain district, only a short distance from the city.

"The object was seen by several people, including two local policemen and a minerals expert named John Edmunds.

"Some have said it looked like a giant robot, others that it was more like a walking tank, with enormous treads for feet.

"At the moment nobody can be sure which of these descriptions best fits the unknown object, but we hope to bring you pictures in a short while.

"The object has cut a deep path of destruction through the forest and so far has not been sighted again. In the meantime, the government would like to stress that it is most definitely *not of this world*.

"I repeat—*not of this world*. This object has come from outer space, its origin and purpose unknown.

"You are asked to remain calm, and mountain district people are advised to stay indoors. So far the object seems more intent on escaping detection than on attacking anyone nearby.

"I repeat—if you live in the mountain district

area, *please stay inside your homes,* and stay tuned to this channel for further details.

"At this moment army units are advancing upon the area. They are determined to cordon off the forest containing the alien and evacuate anyone in the vicinity. Then they will close in.

"The army has no intention of attacking the alien unless provoked. Their plan is to try and make contact with the alien, if this is possible, and try and halt its wild path of destruction."

The announcer paused for a moment. He looked down, cleared his throat, and then looked up. He looked even more serious than before. "It is believed that a young boy is trapped inside. Because of this, army units are moving in with great care. . . ."

The news went on like this for some time. When the newsman was finished, a distinguished-looking professor named Foyster spoke briefly.

"We wish to stress that our earnest wish is to make contact with this mechanical creature from another world, and to rescue the boy unharmed.

"We must do everything in our power to make sure that this being does not mistake our intentions. There must be no fighting, no killing. We must make this a test case upon which any future dealings with extraterrestrials are made.

"This will be our first contact with a creature

59

from another world. We must strive to become friends, not enemies. And for all we know it may have weapons far in advance of our own. . . ."

The professor's voice droned on for another few seconds and was then cut off. Stephen and his mother watched, wide-eyed, the images that now flooded the television screen.

Long lines of military vehicles were streaming down the many roads leading into the mountains. The sky swarmed with helicopters, like a great cloud of summer insects.

There appeared on the screen some hurried, blurry pictures Dad had taken in the forest—the ruined trees and something dark and shadowy at the end of the long tunnel.

Stephen wondered where his father was—and where, oh where, was Erik?

7

Erik had been knocked unconscious when the spacesuit had lurched suddenly to its feet.

His head had thumped against the door of the entrance hatch and he had passed out.

It was a long while before he came to. He had missed the great noise and battering as the spacesuit tore away from the clearing. Now he was conscious only of the steady movement of the robot.

He remembered where he was and he could feel the deep and far-off roar of mighty engines.

His head swam. He had never before felt so dizzy in all his life. The spacesuit lurched from side to side, tossing him around like a bale of wheat.

He grabbed hold of the narrow ladder and held on. He tried to think. Where were they going? For that matter, were they still on Earth? Had he been spirited away to some distant world?

The thought terrified him. Never to see his family again! . . .

His lungs burned as though they were on fire. It was hard to think straight. He tried to sit up, and the effort almost made him sick. He didn't seem to have an ounce of energy left. How was he ever going to get out of this mess?

A weak light crept down to the entrance hatch area from the top of the ladder.

Now he remembered. The ladder led up to the great helmeted head of the robot! If he could climb up there, he would be able to look out through the faceplate and get some idea of where they were.

From the constant crashing sounds that accompanied the spacesuit's movement, he imagined they were still making their way through a forest. But would it be like any forest he remembered?

He took a firm grip of the first few rungs of the ladder and began to climb.

Up, up, *up*. A few rungs at a time and then pausing while the waves of giddiness swept over him. It had seemed such a short climb—no more than the height of a very tall man—but already it

seemed that he had been climbing for ages without getting any farther.

He gritted his teeth and pressed on.

If only the robot would stop *moving*! Then it
wouldn't be so bad. . . .

There was an opening ahead of him, only a few
short rungs away. It looked like an oval-shaped

doorway. He wondered what he would find there. Some sort of control room, perhaps? But for *whom?* The unknown master of this giant robot?

While the Earth boy struggled to climb the narrow ladder, Tyro sat huddled in his seat.

There was a worried look on his smooth face. Beyond the faceplate the dark forest kept rushing toward him, only to be struck aside by the rampaging spacesuit.

It was moving like a blind thing, striking out at random and pushing the tall trees aside like straws. It seemed to think there was no other way of making progress through this world!

Its radar eyes could hardly see. It had lost a lot of power because of its mad plunge—and it was losing more every moment! Tyro could do nothing to cancel the mixed-up automatic program the computer was using. The manual controls were useless. All he could hope for was that the motors would collapse or the fuel would be exhausted.

Of course they were many, many miles away from the natives by now, but the path the wild robot had carved would make them easy to find.

Tyro prayed to his gods and hoped the suit would soon stagger to a halt. Then he would be able to examine it carefully himself and, with a bit of luck, make the repairs that the computer had overlooked.

But this was a forlorn hope. Already the air inside the spacesuit was getting stale. In another hour or so he would have to risk mixing it with the alien air of Earth. It was the only way to stretch out his remaining supply. He was prepared to try anything that would help him to keep alive for a few more hours—until the starship returned. If it ever returned. Time was running out for Tyro.

It was at this precise and unexpected moment that he heard a sound behind him. . . .

After what seemed like hours and hours, Erik finally reached the top of the ladder. He dragged himself over the edge and lay across the entrance to the control room, gasping for air.

He lay there like a stranded fish, staring up at a featureless gray ceiling. After a while he managed to make another great effort and sat up.

The floor lurched and shuddered underneath him. He braced himself on all fours and peered straight ahead.

There was a mist before his eyes. He blinked a couple of times and it went away for a moment —long enough for him to look through the enormous faceplate in front of him and see the forest rushing toward him.

He gasped and shrank back in alarm. They were Earth trees, all right, and the robot was plowing through them like a juggernaut!

He appeared to be in a control room of some sort. There were dials and meters and switches directly in front of him, and on his left . . .

Erik froze. He was looking straight into the eyes of the strangest little man he had ever seen. He had a small, shiny head, with no hair at all, and wide, enormous eyes that reminded him of a sad puppy.

Only for a moment was Erik frightened. Then a smile stretched his face. He almost laughed.

Why, he had never expected the occupant of the robot to be so small! He was even smaller than his brother, and he had the saddest face Erik had ever seen.

Watching him, held back in his seat by the large protective webs, the alien looked for all the world like a frightened child.

And to think, Erik mused, *I was so afraid of him!*

The tiny alien looked back at him. His face was white, with a bluish tinge. His hands were folded in his lap. Even though there was nothing they could say to each other that either could understand, Erik, feeling weak and faint, struggled to make some sort of gesture.

"Hi," he mumbled. He held out one hand and almost fell flat on his face. He gave a foolish grin. "My name's . . . Erik. I know . . . you can't understand me. And . . . I'm sure sorry to see you all

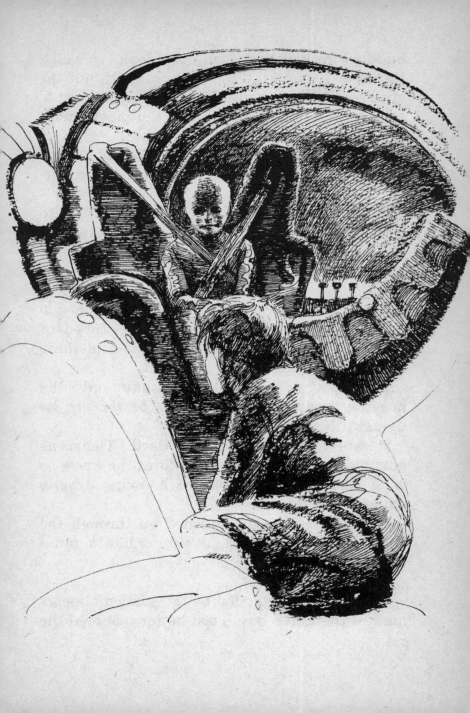

huddled up like that. You don't look . . . well."
He tried to stand up, to steady himself, but the
effort proved impossible.

"Say," he muttered, "what's the matter with
this crazy machine of yours?"

At first the alien regarded him coldly. A universe stretched between them, vast and unfamiliar. And yet . . .

Erik felt the eyes of the alien look deeply into
his, in a way no human being had ever looked.
And he no longer felt alone or afraid. Something
warm passed between them, invisible but strong.
The tiny creature still regarded him without expression, but they seemed to have reached a
common understanding without the need of
words. Perhaps, after all, there *was* something
beyond language.

Erik swayed and collapsed again onto the
heaving, swaying floor. *It must be the air,* he
thought. *It's not like ours. . . .*

He knew they were still on Earth. The scene
outside the faceplate was the forest he knew so
well. But he had no way of knowing *exactly*
where they were.

The robot spacesuit stormed on through the
trees, charging around in circles like a blind
person. . . .

Tyro had been startled by the sudden appearance of the Earth boy. Then he remembered the open hatchway and the strange sounds he had heard.

His feeling of panic gave way to concern when he saw how ill the Earth boy was. *Why,* he realized, *my air must be as bad for him as his is for me!*

Now it became more urgent than ever to bring the spacesuit to a stop so that he could set the boy free.

Without any thought of danger to himself, he unfastened the protective webbing that held him down and climbed out of his seat.

He made his way toward the boy, his tiny hands braced wide apart in case the spacesuit sent him sprawling. With dull eyes, the Earth boy watched him approach.

Tyro's heart hammered painfully. Like the rest of his people, he was small and his bones were easily broken. If he wasn't careful . . .

But he reached the boy unharmed. He kneeled by his side and looked long and deeply into the soft blue eyes which now showed an unhealthy glaze. The boy's cheeks were flushed a deep red and he was breathing heavily.

"Do not worry," Tyro said, in his strange musical speech. "I will find a way to set you free when the spacesuit stops. All will be well. *Trust me. . . .*"

Of course Erik couldn't understand a word of this. But the alien smiled down at him, and Erik smiled back. He was not afraid anymore. They were brothers in distress.

Although the alien was smaller than him, Erik felt that the alien was much older. And indeed he was. Tyro was older than anyone on Earth. His people lived long lives.

Just then the spacesuit gave a sickening lurch to one side.

Tyro braced himself against the floor and looked anxiously at the control panel. If only there was something he could *do*! . . .

Suddenly the faceplate was clear of onrushing trees. There was open sky ahead of them. They were out of the forest at last!

Sunlight streamed into the control room. Tyro sat up and began moving back to his seat. Now there was a chance . . . *if* the computer would only come to its senses and bring the rampaging spacesuit to a halt!

But something went wrong. He had barely moved an inch when the sky abruptly disappeared. The floor of the control room tilted sharply as the giant spacesuit tumbled over. They were falling!

With only seconds in which to act, Tyro made a dive toward the Earth boy. He pinned Erik to the floor and huddled his tiny body around the dazed child, hoping to protect him from the awful crash he knew was coming.

A moment later they hit the ground.

It wasn't as bad as he had expected. The space-suit shuddered and rolled over twice, tossing them around like marbles. Then it growled and was still.

Tyro held his breath for a long moment; then he opened his eyes. The spacesuit was resting at a crazy angle, nearly facedown on the ground. All he could see through the faceplate was the dark-ness of the alien soil pressed against the glass.

Luckily the fall had been only a short one. Tyro was a little bruised, and so was the Earth boy, but no bones had been broken. The little alien breathed a deep sigh of relief.

The air hurt his lungs.

Tyro frowned and took another deep breath. Sure enough, the air felt different and not at all pleasant to breathe.

His spacesuit was strong, but there was a limit to the amount of punishment it could take. First the long fall through the sky and then the tre-mendous crash through the forest. And now this fall. Why, it must have cracked in several places . . . and the alien air of Earth was already creep-ing inside. . . .

The Earth boy was rousing. He managed to sit up and prop himself against the wall. His eyes wandered around the mysterious control room, always coming back to where Tyro crouched before the faceplate.

A dead weight settled around the alien's shoulders. The same air that bit deep into his lungs and stung his eyes had begun to bring some life back to the Earth boy.

Tyro shook his head sadly. What a strange pair they were. . . .

But there was no time to waste! This was the opportunity he had been waiting for. The fall had brought the spacesuit to a stop. If he could get the entrance hatch open, then the boy could get back to his people. . . .

Tyro reached out and pulled the lever on the control panel that worked the hatch. He waited for a moment, but nothing happened. There was no soft whir of machinery to let him know that the entrance had opened. It was still tightly closed.

Whatever was he going to do? He knew that there was another way out of the spacesuit. But that could only be used in case of an emergency, and certainly not while the spacesuit lay with its head on the ground. It would be much too dangerous to risk. So . . .

There was nothing he could do.

There was a growling underneath them. The spacesuit stirred into life. In a moment the short-lived opportunity to escape was gone. The spacesuit roared and struggled to its feet. It made a noise like a thousand broken bearings and took off suddenly at a terrific pace—in no particular direction.

Tyro was thrown back into his seat. The protective webbing snapped automatically into place, pinning him back. Erik rolled around on the floor, trying to find something to hang on to.

This is crazy, he thought. *Whatever am I doing here? And who is that strange little man?* The air inside the spacesuit had fogged his memory. But it was gradually coming back. Fresh air was creeping in through the cracked shell of the spacesuit, prodding him back to full awareness.

To Tyro the situation looked hopeless. The spacesuit was wildly out of control and there was nothing he could do to stop it. The worst that could happen would be for them to be smashed to pieces when the blind spacesuit blundered into a mountainside . . . or crashed into a ravine. That would stop it. But it might also kill them both.

Erik managed to stand up and support himself by leaning against the back of Tyro's heavily padded control seat. He tried to push aside his fear and talk to the alien. But his words came out all mixed up, like a baby's.

He tried to tell the strange little man that he wanted to get out, that he was sorry to have crept inside, and that his family would be wondering where he was. A part of him knew the alien would not have been able to understand his words, even if they had not been so garbled. But Tyro reached up and placed a warm hand over his, and Erik knew that something, at least, had been understood. But there seemed to be nothing the alien could do to stop the headlong rush of the enormous spacesuit.

Tyro's face was sad. "I am sorry," he said. "I did not mean this to happen. I have done what I could. . . ." His strange, musical words drifted away into silence. He looked straight ahead, through the faceplate, with a hopeless expression. He had forgotten all about home and the starship. This terrible plight had stripped such thoughts from his mind. All that mattered was waiting for the end.

From the angle of the floor, Tyro could tell they were moving steadily uphill. The climb had slowed the spacesuit down. If the slope became too steep it might stop the engines . . . or so the alien hoped. Already he could hear the motors working hard to make the climb.

There were houses in the distance—straight ahead, on the crest of a hill. The spacesuit churned steadily toward them. Tyro flinched when he realized there would be a steep drop on the other side.

This is almost the end, he thought. *Soon it will crash and we will probably both be killed. What a strange way to die! I never expected . . .*

Something moved outside. Overhead, in the brilliant blue sky. A number of dark insects were following the path of the robot.

Tyro blinked—and looked again. No, these were not insects, he realized. They looked like flying machines. . . .

One of them swooped close enough for the spacesuit to have raised one huge hand and touched it . . . or smashed it out of the sky.

The aircraft had no wings, only a madly spinning propeller on top. Inside the cabin Tyro could see strange white faces staring down at him. They looked frightened.

Another swooped down. Then another. The sky seemed to be filled with them, swirling around him like gigantic black insects.

The people of Earth had finally found him!

8

Several hours had passed since the spaceman had fallen to Earth. By now satellites had carried the news to every corner of the globe. People sat wide-eyed in front of their television sets or listened to their portable radios. The last moments of the fallen spaceman were witnessed by millions of people.

Stephen and his mother watched with them, waiting to hear if Erik had been saved, or if he had been lost forever.

Dad was out there, somewhere—working along with the army and the air force, trying to find his son. They had seen him on the television a couple of times, talking with some scientists.

All roads leading into the mountain district had been blocked off. Frightened families had been taken from their homes to places of safety. There was no way of knowing where the giant robot would break through next and smash their dwellings into matchwood.

A team of helicopter pilots finally spotted the wild robot. It was heading toward a tourist valley.

The pilots radioed this information to the people on the ground. The army closed in. Everyone held their breath, wondering what would happen.

A few brave pilots flew in close to the fast-moving spaceman. They tried to make radio contact with whoever was inside, but, of course, it was useless. Even if Tyro had been able to use his own communications set, they would not have been able to understand his words.

Tyro gazed through bleary eyes at the worried faces of the men inside the helicopters. He wanted to tell them that he *would* not and *could* not harm them, that it was not in his nature to harm any living thing.

In this way, Tyro and his people were most unlike us. They were the most peaceful race in all the universe. Many years ago, when the Earth was young, they had learned to live in peace with each other. They loved and honored every life form.

One of the helicopters swung suddenly away from the advancing giant. The pilot radioed desperately to the people waiting below.

"The lake! The lake! That crazy thing is heading straight for the lake. . . . !"

The spacesuit crossed the crest of the hill without crashing blindly through any of the houses. It plunged straight ahead and down the other side.

The slope was not very steep, but the spacesuit roared forward at a breakneck pace. A wide, blue lake glimmered in the sunlight, only a little way ahead.

Tyro leaned forward. An expression of hope appeared in his dull eyes. He watched the great bowl of water rushing toward them and closed his eyes and prayed.

Erik sat up. He was finding it possible to think clearly again.

"What's happening?" he asked. He tried to stand up, but he was still too weak. He managed to rise up to his knees and then leaned against the wall for support.

Tyro didn't seem to notice him. The alien was intent upon what was happening outside, beyond the grimy faceplate.

Tyro was wondering how deep the lake was.

Would it be shallow enough for the spacesuit to continue across to the other side, or would it swallow it up?

Erik managed to crawl over to the control panel. He tried to raise himself enough to look out through the faceplate, but he didn't have enough strength.

The alien placed a warm hand on his shoulder. His big, dark eyes were filled with tears. How strange, Erik thought. He really trusted this odd little man. There was nothing frightening about him at all. . . .

"You must be brave," Tyro said. His words came out in a dry squeak. But there was nothing more he could say. The end was near.

They hit the water with a mighty splash. The spacesuit threw up a great wave on either side as it plunged into the lake. It surged forward without hesitation, leaving behind a huge wake.

Soon the water reached halfway up the sides of the spacesuit and continued to rise. But at the same time, Tyro could sense them slowing down. He almost smiled with relief and squeezed the Earth boy's arm.

The deep water was acting like a brake. The headlong plunge of the spacesuit had slowed almost to a standstill. The farther it advanced into the deep water, the slower it moved.

This was just what Tyro had hoped for! The motors were laboring under the strain. Any moment now they might stop altogether . . . and they would be saved!

But the water continued to rise. Up past the blackened waist of the spacesuit, creeping toward the armpits.

They still moved sluggishly through the water. Strange growling noises filled the cabin. With a shock, Tyro realized that the spacesuit was beginning to break up—the pressure of the water on the open cracks was causing it to collapse.

The spacesuit floundered another few yards into the lake and then came to a stop. Dark, muddy water swirled underneath the raised arms. Small waves lapped against the side of the stalled giant. It stood motionless, staring toward a shore it would now never reach.

Tyro's relief was short-lived. The spacesuit had been stopped all right. But they were stuck fast in the middle of a large lake—how were they ever going to escape now?

Far below Tyro could hear the spacesuit filling with water. It was only a matter of time before the damaged panels would give way and they would sink beneath the waves.

There was only one thing he could do—save the Earth boy. He could use the emergency exit now, even though he knew such an action might

cost him his life. But . . . *the child must be saved.*
These people must never think unkindly of my
people, Tyro thought.

The little alien climbed down from his seat. He
motioned to Erik to follow him, then went over
to the oval doorway leading down to the entrance hatch.

He pointed to the ladder, smiling. "We have to
go down there," he said, knowing the boy would
not understand his words, but hoping he would
understand his meaning. "It won't be for long.
And do not be afraid of what you will find
there. . . ."

To Erik it seemed that the alien was directing
him out of the spacesuit. He remembered where
the entrance doorway had been, and the narrow
ladder leading down. He smiled and nodded his
thanks and began climbing down.

The floor of the hatch area was covered with
water. It was six inches deep and rising rapidly.
All around him the metal of the spacesuit
groaned and shuddered.

Erik looked back in alarm. Tyro, at the top of
the ladder, smiled and motioned him along. Only
the alien knew he was putting on a brave face.
His vision was so blurred he could barely see,
and his movements were like those of a drunken
man as he forced himself to climb down the
82

ladder through the muddled air, a mixture of his own sweet atmosphere and the aching air of Earth.

I must not let him see I am so ill, he kept thinking. *For if he does, then I fear he will panic. . . .*

They reached the floor of the hatch area. The chilly water lapped halfway up Erik's legs. He shivered and turned to the little alien for directions.

Tyro pressed a large black lever near the ladder. It was an emergency device, quite simple and effective, that operated independently of the rest of the spacesuit.

Tyro made a sign that they were to huddle down, as close together as possible.

The water touched their thighs and rose toward their waists. They waited.

Erik heard a number of small explosions. They went off one after the other, like firecrackers. He felt the spacesuit give a great lurch and he was sure they were going to topple over. But when the roar had died away he was pleased to see that the floor had only a slight list.

Erik gasped. A great wave of fresh air came roaring down from the control room. It was the coolest, most beautiful breeze he had ever known.

The wave of air sent Tyro reeling. He almost blacked out with the pain. He struggled to remain standing and motioned to the Earth boy to climb the ladder.

Erik obeyed. The shock of the explosions had forced open the entrance hatch a few inches, and water was pouring in. But there was no escape in that direction.

He climbed.

Tyro reeled after him, grasping at the tiny rungs of the ladder with weak fingers. But they caught . . . and held! He began the agonizing task of following the Earth boy up the ladder and back into the control room.

Erik helped him up the last few steps and hauled him out into the control room. The little alien's body was limp and exhausted. He seemed barely alive.

Erik felt a breeze tugging at him. He looked up and around, his eyes widening with surprise.

The walls of the cabin had disappeared! All he could see was the familiar blue sky and water spreading out around them.

Anxious helicopters circled overhead. Only a few seconds earlier the pilots had cried out in alarm when the great helmeted head of the spacesuit had suddenly blasted skyward, narrowly missing some of them. It had screamed up into the sky like a rocket, and when the smoke

had cleared behind it they found themselves looking down into what looked like the control room of some strange machine. Something stirred down there . . . and waved to them.

It was Erik. He breathed the sweet, fresh air of his own world and waved like mad, hoping they would see him.

The little alien lay at his feet, unconscious. For all Erik knew he might even have been dead, killed by the air he could not share. All that mattered was to bring help as fast as he could. His eyes filled with tears when he remembered how Tyro had tried to save his life. He had been such a good friend.

There was a roar close by and he could feel the air beating down on him savagely. One of the helicopters had come dangerously close. A moment later it was hovering directly overhead. A door swung open and a rope ladder came tumbling down. The end of it dangled a little to Erik's right, just in front of the control panel.

A man appeared and began to climb down the wildly swaying rungs. He looked like some sort of soldier. Erik watched him climb down, shielding his eyes against the sun, and drop onto the listing floor of the control room. Carrying a pistol in his right hand, he looked quickly around. He saw the stricken alien in the corner and relaxed slightly. Then he swung toward Erik.

"Come on," he said. "Up the ladder. *Quick*. I'll be right behind you. Don't be frightened. . . ."

Erik nodded toward Tyro. "What . . . what about him?"

The soldier flicked his head impatiently toward the swaying ladder. "Worry about him—that—later. My orders are to get you out of here, that's all. Come on, I'll show you how. . . ."

The ladder swayed dangerously as they climbed. Only once did Erik look back, and it seemed that the little alien had roused himself. For a moment their eyes met, and a great sadness passed between them. Tyro raised one weak arm in a gesture of farewell. Then he fell back against the wall and was still.

Erik's eyes blurred with tears and he clung to the swaying ladder. He knew he would never forget the strange little man and the marvelous adventure they had had.

Below him the soldier prodded him gently. "Come on. Keep moving. Only a few feet to go. . . ."

They made it. And when he was safe aboard the helicopter, he looked down for the last time at what was left of the giant spacesuit.

It looked strange, standing in the water with its head blown off and most of it hidden below the water. It was listing heavily to one side as the lake slowly pulled it down.

The helicopter swung away, toward the shore,

where hundreds of people were waiting. His father would be among them. Erik brightened when he realized what a wonderful story he would have to tell. But now and again he thought of Tyro, and his face grew sad. He wondered whatever would become of him, and if there was still time to rescue him from the sinking spacesuit. . . .

9

Tyro watched the helicopter disappear from view. Soon the sky was empty. There was only the great circle of blue sky hanging over him.

He made an enormous effort and crawled to the other side of the control room and looked out across the water.

His vision was blurred, but he could make out the dim figures of the many people lining the distant shore. The strange wind of Earth lapped at his face and drove his thoughts away. It was difficult to think. His blood was on fire.

How long? he wondered. How long could he remain alive in this atmosphere . . . and did it matter? It was only a matter of moments now before the spacesuit toppled over and took him beneath the waves.

He felt sad. This was such an absurd way to end his life. To sink to the bottom of a deep lake on a world he had never called home?

Dimly he could make out a number of small boats circling around the doomed spacesuit. He was overcome with a sudden desire to sleep . . . and to forget the pain cutting deeply into his flesh.

If only . . . *if only* . . . He fell back onto the floor, eyes glazing over.

There was no one to help him. But he had done his best—he had saved the Earth boy. They would not think badly of him, these people of Earth. Perhaps they would remember him if his people ever passed this way again. . . .

His world grew gradually darker. He could hear his own heartbeat hammering with the solemn approach of death.

You have done well, he thought, deep in the dark mist of his dying. He nodded to himself, smiling. Death was very near.

And then he wondered, *Had that been a thought?* No, it had seemed more like a voice . . . a voice inside his head saying:

YOU HAVE DONE WELL, TYRO.

There—there could be no mistaking it! It was the voice of one of his people, calling directly to his mind. Why, even now it was sounding out over the lake and sending ripples racing toward the shore!

YOU HAVE DONE WELL, TYRO, AND NOW WE SHALL TAKE YOU HOME....

Hope returned. He could not believe it! They had come back for him at last. They had found him! They had not forgotten him and the starship *had* returned....

Suddenly a great silence fell over the world. The waves were stilled and the lake became as smooth as glass. Nothing moved for miles around. Communications ceased. The watchers on the shore were frozen like wax dummies, unable to move, able only to stare in wonder.

A powerful force field held the land in thrall. Small boats drifted lifelessly on the lake, their motors stilled. Helicopters stalled and then idled gently to a landing.

A great golden light blossomed over the lake. Through it Tyro could see the shadowy shape of the starship come to take him home. His heart swelled with happiness.

The watchers on the shore saw nothing. They could feel something strange happening on the lake, but the starship's field of invisibility made sure they saw nothing else. And all around them the air tingled strangely, alive with a powerful force field.

Tyro could feel the great power reaching out for him. And he smiled. He felt happy again. It was good to be going home.

The spacesuit moved under him. It broke free of the mud and the lake and rose high above the water. It moved swiftly toward the great golden cloud hiding the starship, drawn to it by the powerful magnetic force reaching out across the lake.

The people on the shore watched open-mouthed as it came clear of the lake. It looked like a headless diving suit flying through the air! The great helmet now lay at the bottom of the lake. In time scientists would salvage it and study it. But for the moment all eyes were on the strange spectacle of the flying spacesuit. . . .

To the watchers on the shore it seemed that the dark blur of the spacesuit suddenly entered a glittering shaft of sunlight . . . and disappeared.

Moments later the air ceased to tingle and they were released from their frozen state. Motors roared into life and people looked at each other in an embarrassed silence. Where had the space-man gone?

But even as they asked this question, Tyro was very far away. The great entrance hatch of the starship had thrown wide its arms and taken him inside, where loving hands took care of him and eased away his pain.

92

93

Later, when the starship sped away from Earth, he watched wistfully as the planet fell away beneath him. It looked more beautiful than ever now that he was safe and back in his own world. Perhaps he would return one day, and see how things had changed.

He thought of all that had happened to him—his dreadful fall and the nightmarish ride inside the damaged spacesuit—and his promise did not waver. For it seemed to him that his people had made a mistake. The people of Earth were not as warlike as they had been made to seem. The children were kind and helpful, and there was much hope for the future with the little people of Earth. He made a mental note to tell the scientists that they had studied Earth from too great a distance, that they should have been much closer.

Yes, he would return to Earth. But not for a while. Not until their wars had ended and the people of that blue world were brothers. And that might take some time. The people of Earth were confused and afraid, but in their children there was hope for a happier world. Tyro felt sure of that. And one day . . . *one day* . . .

The Earth grew smaller and smaller below. It was soon lost among the stars. Fast and faster sped the starship, moving like a great bird of space, its wings spread wide across the dark ocean of the universe. And it was carrying him closer and closer to the traveling space city of his people.

Tyro was going home.

ABOUT THE AUTHOR

LEE HARDING lives in the mountains of Australia, not too far from the city of Melbourne. Many of his science-fiction novels have been published in Australia, England, and the U.S., as have the various science-fiction collections he has edited. He has also published more than forty science-fiction short stories, which have been translated into nine languages. His novel *Misplaced Persons* won the 1978 Alan Marshall Award.

ABOUT THE ILLUSTRATORS

JOHN SCHOENHERR studied at the Art Students League and Pratt Institute. He has won a Hugo Award for his science-fiction illustrations. His son, IAN, is a talented young artist, who has won several regional awards for his work. The Schoenherrs live on a farm in New Jersey.

☐ **MISS KNOW IT ALL**   15408/$2.25

☐ **MISS KNOW IT ALL RETURNS**   15351/$2.25
by Carol Beach York
Miss Know It All appears suddenly one morning on the door-stop of the Good Day Home for Girls. All 28 girls are amazed at all Miss Know It All knows. But something happens to make the girls fear that they will lose their wonderful Miss Know It All forever! Both these warm and delightful books must reading.

☐ **DOWNTOWN FAIRY**   15386/$1.95
GODMOTHER
by Charlotte Pomerantz
"If only," wishes Olivia, "I had a fairy godmother!" Suddenly out of a glimmer of blue light a plump woman with sparkling blue eyes appears. Olivia now has her fairy grandmother who immediately makes her invisible, and takes her on a fabulous adventure that changes Olivia's life forever.

☐ **HELP, THERE'S A CAT**   15374/$2.50
WASHING IN HERE
by Alison Smith
Henry Walker has a choice: he can keep house for his youn-ger brother and sister while his mother is busy or else horrible Aunt Wilhelmina will come to stay. Henry decides to take charge, but he wasn't prepared for Kitty, a 20-pound yellow-eyed monster cat.

☐ JACOB TWO-TWO MEETS THE HOODED FANG

42109/$2.50

by Mordechai Richler

Jacob Two-Two says everything twice because no one listens to him the first time. But then he is convicted of insulting a grown-up and exiled to Slimer's Isle—a nightmarish prison guarded by wolverines and slithering snakes and the dreaded Hooded Fang!

☐ OWLS IN THE FAMILY

15350/$2.25

by Farley Mowat

This is the hilarious true tale of two Saskatchewan owls; Wol is a wonderful bird who terrorizes everyone, and Weeps is a comical bird afraid of almost everything, except a dog named Mutt. There are laughs galore as these two shake up a neighborhood, turn a house topsy-turvy and even outsmart Mutt!

☐ ARTHUR THE KID

15169/$2.25

by Alan Coren

When the bumbling Black Hand Gang, the gofiest outlaws in the Wild West, advertise for a boss, who do they get? Arthur the Kid, of course!

Match Wits with America's
Sherlock Holmes in
Sneakers

ENCYCLOPEDIA BROWN

With a head full of facts and his
eyes and ears on the world of
Idaville, meet Leroy (Encyclo-
pedia) Brown. Each Encyclope-
dia Brown book contains 10 baf-
fling cases to challenge, stymie
and amuse young sleuths. Best
of all, the reader can try solving
each case on his own before
looking up the solution in the
back of the book. "BRIGHT
AND ENTERTAINING. . . ."
The New York Times
By Donald Sobol

☐ 15359	ENCYCLOPEDIA BROWN BOY DETECTIVE #1	$2.25
☐ 15392	ENCYCLOPEDIA BROWN/CASE OF THE SECRET PITCH #2	$2.25
☐ 15177	ENCYCLOPEDIA BROWN FINDS THE CLUE #3	$2.25
☐ 15526	ENCYCLOPEDIA BROWN GETS HIS MAN #4	$2.50
☐ 15404	ENCYCLOPEDIA BROWN KEEPS THE PEACE #6	$2.25
☐ 15539	ENCYCLOPEDIA BROWN SAVES THE DAY #7	$2.50
☐ 15525	ENCYCLOPEDIA BROWN TRACKS THEM DOWN #8	$2.50
☐ 15393	ENCYCLOPEDIA BROWN SHOWS THE WAY #9	$2.25
☐ 15423	ENCYCLOPEDIA BROWN TAKES THE CASE #10	$2.25
☐ 15371	ENCYCLOPEDIA BROWN & THE CASE OF THE MIDNIGHT VISITOR #13	$2.25
☐ 15352	ENCYCLOPEDIA BROWN AND THE MYSTERIOUS HANDPRINTS #16	$2.25

Prices and availability subject to change without notice.

More Fun More Adventure More Magic

CHOOSE YOUR OWN ADVENTURE

SKYLARK EDITIONS

☐	15226	Jungle Safari #13 E. Packard	$1.95
☐	15442	The Search For Champ #14 S. Gilligan	$2.25
☐	15444	Three Wishes #15 S. Gilligan	$2.25
☐	15465	Dragons! #16 J. Razzi	$2.25
☐	15489	Wild Horse Country #17 L. Sonberg	$2.25
☐	15262	Summer Camp #18 J. Gitenstein	$1.95
☐	15490	The Tower of London #19 S. Saunders	$2.25
☐	15501	Trouble In Space #20 J. Woodcock	$2.25
☐	15283	Mona Is Missing #21 S. Gilligan	$1.95
☐	15418	The Evil Wizard #22 A. Packard	$2.25
☐	15306	The Flying Carpet #25 J. Razzi	$1.95
☐	15318	The Magic Path #26 J. Goodman	$1.95
☐	15467	Ice Cave #27 Saunders/Packard	$2.25
☐	15342	The Fairy Kidnap #29 S. Gilligan	$1.95
☐	15463	Runaway Spaceship #30 S. Saunders	$2.25
☐	15508	Lost Dog! #31 R. A. Montgomery	$2.25
☐	15379	Blizzard of Black Swan #32 Saunders/Packard	$2.25
☐	15380	Haunted Harbor #33 S. Gilligan	$2.25
☐	15399	Attack of the Monster Plants #34 S. Saunders	$2.25
☐	15416	Miss Liberty Caper #35 S. Saunders	$2.25
☐	15449	The Owl Tree #36 R. A. Montgomery	$2.25
☐	15453	Haunted Halloween Party #37 S. Saunders	$2.25
☐	15458	Sand Castle #38 R. A. Montgomery	$2.25
☐	15477	Caravan #39 R. A. Montgomery	$2.25
☐	15492	The Great Easter Bunny Adventure #40 E. Packard	$2.25
☐	15509	The Movie Mystery #41 S. Saunders	$2.25

Prices and availability subject to change without notice.

Bantam Skylark Paperbacks
The Kid-Pleasers

Especially designed for easy reading with large type, wide margins and captivating illustrations, Skylarks are "kid-pleasing" paperbacks featuring the authors, subjects and characters children love.

☐	15258	**BANANA BLITZ** Florence Parry Heide	$2.25
☐	15259	**FREAKY FILLINS #1** David Hartley	$1.95
☐	15250	**THE GOOD-GUY CAKE** Barbara Dillion	$1.95
☐	15381	**C.L.U.T.Z.** Marilyn Wilkes	$2.25
☐	15384	**MUSTARD** Charlotte Graeber	$2.25
☐	15157	**ALVIN FERNALD: TV ANCHORMAN** Clifford Hicks	$1.95
☐	15338	**ANASTASIA KRUPNIK** Lois Lowry	$2.50
☐	15168	**HUGH PINE** Janwillen Van de Wetering	$1.95
☐	15248	**CHARLIE AND THE CHOCOLATE FACTORY** Roald Dahl	$2.50
☐	15174	**CHARLIE AND THE GREAT GLASS ELEVATOR** Roald Dahl	$2.50
☐	15317	**JAMES AND THE GIANT PEACH** Roald Dahl	$2.95
☐	15255	**ABEL'S ISLAND** William Steig	$2.25
☐	15194	**BIG RED** Jim Kjelgaard	$2.50
☐	15206	**IRISH RED: SON OF BIG RED** Jim Kjelgaard	$2.25
☐	01803	**JACOB TWO-TWO MEETS THE HOODED FANG** Mordecai Richler	$2.95
☐	15343	**THE TWITS** Roald Dahl	$2.50

Prices and availability subject to change without notice.

Buy them at your local bookstore or use this handy coupon for ordering:

Shop at home
for quality childrens books
and save money, too.

Now you can order books for the whole family from Bantam's latest listing of hundreds of titles including many fine children's books. *And* this special offer gives you an opportunity to purchase a Bantam book for only 50¢. Here's how:

By ordering any five books at the regular price per order, you can also choose any other single book listed (up to $4.95 value) for just 50¢. Some restrictions do apply, so for further details send for Bantam's listing of titles today.